Contents

Savage Seas

A fisherman's life is tough. The hours are long and the work is hard. Waves can sweep you overboard. A rope or steel cable can wrap around your legs and drag you under. Then there's the danger from collisions with other boats, explosions, fires on board...

▼ *Cold, wet, gruelling work: battling with gale-force winds, trawlermen haul nets on board an Atlantic fishing boat.*

When the weather gets rough, the tough go fishing. In September 1991, Captain Billy Tyne set off from the port of Gloucester, Massachusetts, on the eastern seaboard of the USA, in his boat the *Andrea Gail*. The weather was good but the fishing was poor. So Captain Tyne took a risk and sailed far out in the Atlantic Ocean.

Into the storm

Things were looking good. Soon the *Andrea Gail* had a hold full of fresh fish. Then the ice machine broke down. The only way to stop the fish from rotting was to hurry to shore. A huge storm was brewing, but the crew agreed to head back to port.

Giant waves

Bravely, Captain Tyne and his crew battled through the stormy seas. But they didn't stand a chance. The waves were taller than a 10-storey house. In the end, the *Andrea Gail* capsized and its six-man crew were never seen again. Captain Tyne's final words on the radio were: 'She's comin' on, boys, and she's comin' on strong!'

MAYDAY! MAYDAY!

Lifeboat crews risk their lives to answer distress calls from ships at sea. In 1981, a lifeboat from Penlee in Cornwall in the UK went to the aid of a ship that was being blown onto the rocks by 18-metre-high waves. In the huge seas, 16 sailors lost their lives, including all eight members of the lifeboat crew.

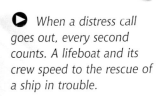

▶ When a distress call goes out, every second counts. A lifeboat and its crew speed to the rescue of a ship in trouble.

Death in the Forest

On the Indonesian island of Sumatra, loggers are clearing tropical rainforest. Driven by poverty and operating outside the law, the men work deep in the jungle – and every day brings the risk of accident, injury or worse…

▶ *Few people choose a job this tough: times are hard in Sumatra and it's the only way these men can feed their families.*

Illegal tree-cutters slave away in the hot, rainy jungles of Sumatra. They work on steep hillsides, in all weathers, often living in the forest for weeks at a time.

Snakes and tigers

By day, the tree thieves chop down the giant trees and send them floating downriver. At night, the crews sleep in a covered platform two metres off the ground to avoid attacks by snakes and tigers.

In 2003, one crew of four had spent a long day cutting trees with chainsaws and were camped deep in the jungle. Three of the loggers rested on the platform, while Siadul, the fourth, cooked the food below.

Caught like a rat

Siadul was sitting on the ground eating his dinner when a hungry Sumatran tiger sprang out of the darkness. He jumped onto Siadul's back, tore out a chunk of flesh and began dragging him away.

His friends bravely fired up their chainsaws to scare the tiger away. But it was too late. Siadul died a few hours later. 'It was like a cat catching a rat,' said Siadul's friend Ponimin.

▼ As forests are cleared to make way for palm oil plantations, Sumatran tigers have become an endangered species. Only a few hundred now survive in the wild.

TIGER ATTACK!

Tigers are not normally man-eaters but will attack humans if they cannot catch other prey. Most man-eaters are either sick or old. Almost all are eventually captured, poisoned or shot.

Buried Alive!

Mining really is a '3D' job: Dirty, Dangerous and Difficult. There's danger everywhere – from fires, poison gas and cave-ins to gas explosions and flooding. Just breathing in coal dust can clog a miner's lungs and cause fatal diseases years afterwards.

◀ Cramped conditions, deafening noise, lethal dust and gases: who'd be a miner?

Jobs don't get much more risky than working in a Chinese coal mine. Many mines in China are illegal and employ migrant workers on pitifully low wages. The miners are forced to do back-breaking, dangerous work in order to send money home. Getting coal out of the ground is everything. Workers' safety counts for nothing.

Trapped

On 15 June 2009, the Xinqiao mine in southwestern China suddenly flooded, trapping 16 miners far below ground. Amazingly, three of them survived for 25 days by eating coal dust and licking water off the walls of the mine.

Rescue at last

Just when they had given up hope, they caught sight of the rescue team's flashlights. The men shouted wildly, 'Hey, over here!' After hearing their calls for help through the rock and mud, the searchers found the pit where they lay. The men were lucky. In 2008, over 3,200 people died in Chinese mines.

DANGER – GAS!

Gas explosions usually cause the worst mining disasters. In November 1963, more than 450 workers were killed when an explosion ripped through a coal mine in Japan, collapsing the roof and filling the mine with deadly carbon monoxide.

◄ Chinese mines have the worst safety record in the world. This miner has been rescued after a gas leak killed 21 of his workmates in a coal mine in central China.

Skywalkers

Next time you're walking around a city, take a look up. High above you, some amazing acrobats are at work. For these skilled workers, manoeuvring girders into position hundreds of metres above street level is all in a day's work.

▼ *Eighty-eight floors up, a 'skywalker' checks the position of a steel girder during construction of the World Financial Center in Shanghai, China.*

'We have as much fear as the next guy'

In 1886, the Canadian Grand Trunk Railway company wanted to build a bridge over the mighty St Lawrence River. They hired a group of local Mohawk Indians, all teenagers. The employers were amazed at how well they coped with heights despite the raging river below. The team was given a nickname: the 'Fearless Wonders'.

Word spread. From the 1920s onwards, Mohawks from the Kahnawake reservation were hired to help build many of New York's most famous skyscrapers, including the Empire State Building, the Chrysler Building, the George Washington Bridge and the World Trade Center. Mohawks are still at work on the city's high buildings today.

Sign language

As well as speaking their own language, Mohawk construction workers invented a special sign language to pass messages quickly and clearly. Not a bad idea when the wind is swirling around you and you're trying to keep your balance on a narrow steel beam, 200 metres up in the air!

'A lot of people think Mohawks aren't afraid of heights; that's not true. We have as much fear as the next guy. The difference is that we deal with it better. We also have the experience of the old timers to follow and the responsibility to lead the younger guys. There's pride in "walking iron".'

Kyle Karonhiaktatie Beauvais
(Mohawk, Kahnawake)

⊙ Photographed in 1970 during the building of a Park Avenue skyscraper, Mohawk Walter Joe Goodleaf is one of six generations of Mohawks who have shaped the New York skyline.

Holy Smoke Jumpers!

Fighting fires is tricky enough. There's danger everywhere, from leaping flames and suffocating smoke to collapsing buildings. Smoke jumpers go one step further. They fight the fires that other fire crews can't reach – by jumping out of a plane!

▼ *Ducking low to protect himself from the intense heat, a firefighter radios for help during a raging forest fire in Spain.*

'Giant orange flames lick the air...'

The door opens. The roar of the air rushing past fills the plane. Below, a fire a kilometre wide is raging. Giant orange flames lick the air. The eight-person firefighting team make a last-minute check on equipment. The plane climbs to the required height and the team step closer to the door, their hearts pounding.

'Get ready!' shouts the team leader. One by one, the men and women hurl themselves out of the door. For a few seconds, they hurtle to the ground at 150 kmh. One by one, the parachutes billow open.

Fighting the fire

Luckily, no one has smashed into a rock or got hung up in a tree. The smoke jumpers go to work. They dig trenches or cut down burning trees to stop the fire from spreading.

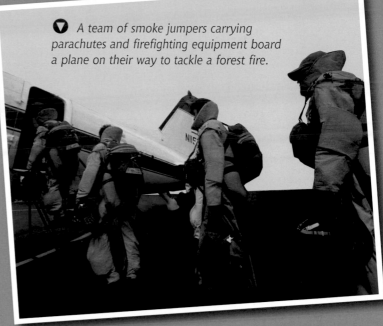

A team of smoke jumpers carrying parachutes and firefighting equipment board a plane on their way to tackle a forest fire.

They have to keep their wits about them. Fires spread with lightning speed. The wind can change direction in an instant. It's hot, sweaty work. Even if the team beat the blaze, there's still the long walk out of the forest carrying pickaxes, chainsaws and other heavy equipment.

RUN FOR YOUR LIFE!

Fires called 'gobblers' devour everything in their path. When the flames are this fierce, the firefighters' only chance is to hide under a special heatproof blanket and pray the fire passes overhead.

Seabed Rescue

When you're working 1,000 metres below the waves, the pressure of the water is the same as a cow standing on your thumbnail. It's harder to move about here than in outer space. And deadly hazards lie in wait on the ocean bed …

Forward-mounted video camera for scientific survey work

Hull built to withstand tons of crushing pressure

▶ *Using its powerful searchlights to pierce the gloom, a deep-sea mini-sub carries out scientific research on the ocean bed.*

Remote-controlled manipulator arm to collect samples from the seabed

Searchlights illuminate the seafloor

August 2005. The Russian mini-sub *Priz* is 190 metres down in the waters off the eastern coast of Siberia. Suddenly, there is a terrible grinding noise. The propeller has become snared in some old fishing nets. The sub is trapped.

Inside, the seven crew members look at each other grimly. It's far too deep to swim to the surface. All they can do is to wait for help from above – or face certain death. There's little to drink or eat and the temperature soon drops to a bone-numbing 6°C.

The rescue

The first rescue attempt by a Russian naval vessel fails. But there's still hope. A British team and their remote-controlled *Scorpio* rescue sub are flying across the world. By the time they arrive, the sailors have been trapped for 72 hours in the *Priz*. In just a few hours, they will run out of air.

The *Scorpio* finds the *Priz* in the cold, dark waters. Its robotic arms cut through the tangle of nets trapping the sub. Soon both subs are back on the surface and all seven crew members are safe.

SUBMARINE HAZARDS

On a mini-sub conditions are cramped and food, water and oxygen are limited. Working at this depth tests the skills, nerves and endurance of the crew to the limit.

Nuclear submarines spend weeks, even months at sea. The crew train constantly to handle emergencies such as fire or flood. As well as maintaining combat readiness, drills help to pass the time.

🔻 *With space on board for 16 persons, this British LR5 sub is specially designed for rescuing crew from stranded or trapped submarines on the ocean bed.*

Flying Daredevils

In the past, pilots were daredevils. They took big risks to break flying records and push themselves and their machines to the limit. Today's flying daredevils don't take such chances – but once in a while, things can still go badly wrong.

▶ *Acrobatic display teams like the RAF Red Arrows fly incredibly close to each other while performing loops and other stunts at high speed. They're thrilling to watch – but just one tiny mistake can lead to disaster.*

A test pilot's job is one of the most dangerous in aviation. Before any plane takes to the air, it is tested in a simulator. Pilot and technicians make a thorough check of the engine, rudders and flaps. Then it's on to the tricky stuff.

Terrifying

Being in a plane when it stalls and drops out of the air is terrifying. But test pilots deliberately make this happen. They turn off the engines in mid-air to see if they restart easily.

Test pilots also land the plane too fast on wet and icy runways, slamming on the brakes until the tyres melt. They need to make sure the plane will survive if one of the controls fails.

Test pilots need a great 'feel' for flying, so they can solve problems quickly. A new jumbo jet can cost up to £260 million, so a test pilot will only eject as a last resort.

No margin for error

When you're flying at twice the speed of sound, there's no margin for error – and even the most sophisticated modern planes can suffer equipment failure. In March 2009, the pilot of a US F-22 Raptor, the world's most advanced fighter jet, was killed when his plane crashed in the desert in southern California. He had been flying for 21 years.

CHUCK YEAGER, TEST PILOT

Legendary test pilot Chuck Yeager (1923-75) is one of the great names in aviation. The first man to fly at the speed of sound, Yeager broke the sound barrier on 14 October 1947, flying an experimental jet-engined plane at a height of 13,700 metres. As well as outstanding flying skills, Yeager had nerves of steel and went on to break many other flying records.

Space Alert!

Ever wanted to orbit the Earth from ten kilometres up? Or take a walk in space? It sounds like fun, but real-life astronauts living for weeks at zero gravity need physical and mental stamina – and steady nerves…

⬤ An astronaut working on the hull of the International Space Station waves to the camera as the station orbits the Earth.

⬤ The International Space Station is the largest satellite ever to orbit the Earth. It serves as a long-term space research laboratory, and many experiments are carried out there every day.

Photovoltaic cells store energy from the Sun

Centrifuge module, for studying effect of gravity levels on living organisms

Experiment module

It's March 2009. The three astronauts on board the International Space Station hear the radio crackle as a warning comes in from Mission Control. A chunk of space debris – part of an old rocket motor – is heading their way. It's only a centimetre in diameter. Why worry?

But the debris is moving fast – about 32,000 km/h. That's seven times faster than a rifle bullet. In space, this is a 'red alert'. Flying debris can easily punch a hole in the station's hull. The air inside then gets sucked out, killing the crew.

A near miss

The three astronauts scramble into the *Soyuz* rocket, which doubles as a lifeboat. For 10 long minutes they wait, peering nervously out of the window, until the space station commander finally radios down to Mission Control. They all heave a sigh of relief when Mission Control gives the all-clear.

LEAVE IT TO THE ROBOTS

Space junk isn't the only worry for astronauts. Zero gravity weakens bones and muscle and can affect the flow of blood to the brain. There's also the risk of radiation from cosmic rays.

Radiators allow heat generated inside the station to escape safely into space

Remote manipulator arm for lifting and maintenance work

Tick, Tick, Boom!

Bombs are deadly. Not surprisingly, most people run away from them. Bomb disposal experts walk slowly towards them. It's up to them to make bombs safe. Now **that's** a risky job!

▼ This huge unexploded bomb was discovered in a remote part of the northern Ugandan bush. Right: A volunteer seals off the area as the bomb disposal team go to work.

In northern Uganda, lethal debris from the war between the Ugandan military and the rebel Lord's Resistance Army is scattered all around. Unexploded bombs, grenades, and mortars litter the countryside. Dozens of people are injured or killed by them each year.

A clean-up crew of army experts and volunteers is working to clear the land of explosive devices. Today their task is to remove a 230 kg bomb discovered by a local farmer.

Volatile

'It's a big one, air-dropped,' says army captain Tom Bahinda as he stands next to the bomb. Disposal of this kind of device is hugely risky. Unlike landmines, bombs are extremely volatile and may explode at any moment.

After sealing off the area, Tom digs away underneath the bomb and places a small explosive charge. The team retreat to a safe distance.

Set for firing

A massive blast cuts the air and a large plume of smoke rises from the blast site. A huge crater surrounded by blackened trees and undergrowth now marks the bomb site.

Their job done, the team pack up their equipment and move on. 'We enjoy this work,' says one. 'We help protect our brothers and sisters and work for the nation.'

⬤ *Wearing protective headgear, the leader of the bomb squad gets ready to place the explosive charge that will detonate the bomb.*

ROBOT HELPERS

In wealthier countries, remote-control robots are used to investigate and disarm unexploded bombs. Uganda's bomb disposal squad cannot afford such luxuries: they do all their work the dangerous way – by hand.

What's Up, Croc?

Don't be fooled. Wildlife is called 'wild' for a reason. Chimps and orang-utans may look cuddly, but in a bad mood they bite off fingers and rip off arms. Every year, zookeepers and animal handlers are mauled by tetchy tigers and roughed up by cranky crocs.

▼ *Never smile at a crocodile. In Africa and parts of South-East Asia, crocodiles kill hundreds of people every year.*

US animal expert Brady Barr, known as the 'croc doc', has met some of the world's most dangerous animals face to face. 'I worked with crocs for twenty years,' he says. 'But I am scared every time I work with them… I know that if I make a mistake I will die.'

One time Brady slipped out of a boat into the water to get closer to a large Nile crocodile and sank into thick mud up to his waist. He was trapped!

▲ 'Croc Doc' Brady Barr and reptile friend.

Brady recalls, 'The crocodile exploded towards me. I braced myself for attack. Everyone in the boat was screaming. I thought this was it. But instead of attacking me, it went right by me.'

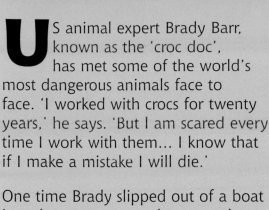

◀ Snakes alive! TV wildlife presenter Steve Irwin shows no fear of this deadly rattlesnake.

'CRIKEY!'

Zoologist Steve Irwin shared his love of animals with millions of TV viewers around the world. He was known for saying 'Crikey!' when things got scary. Sadly, Irwin died in 2006 after being pierced in the chest by a stingray's barb while filming in Australia's Great Barrier Reef.

Man on Wire

Some do it for the money. Some take risks to help others. But there are some rare people – poets, performers, dreamers – who turn danger into art…

'I observed the tightrope dancer – you couldn't call him a "walker" – approximately halfway between the two towers. On seeing us he started to smile and laugh and he started going into a dancing routine on the high wire... He was bouncing up and down. His feet were actually leaving the wire and then he would resettle back on the wire again... Unbelievable really... Everybody was spellbound.'

Eyewitness, Sgt Charles Daniels, NYPD

▼ 'The artistic crime of the century': steadying himself with a balancing pole, high-wire walker Philippe Petit sets out on his death-defying walk between the twin towers of the World Trade Center in New York.

'When I see three oranges, I juggle; when I see two towers, I walk'

Many people dream of achieving fame with a single daring feat, but few set their sights as high as Frenchman Philippe Petit. In 1974, Petit became an overnight celebrity after walking a 417 metre-high wire stretched between the twin towers of New York's World Trade Center.

Planning

Petit's feat is also a story of friend-ship and complicity. It would never have been possible without his best friend, photographer and long-time accomplice, Jean-Louis Blondeau, who planned how to smuggle their equipment past the security guards. Blondeau also worked out how to pass the steel cable across the 43-metre gap between the towers. After six months of preparation they hid in the towers and rigged the wire overnight.

▶ *Born in 1949, Philippe Petit has made dozens of spectacular high-wire performances all over the world. When asked why he chose the Twin Towers, he replied, 'When I see three oranges, I juggle; when I see two towers, I walk.'*

Chatting with seagulls

On 7 August 1974, shortly after 7.15 am, Petit stepped off the South Tower and onto the thin steel cable. Far below on the streets of Manhattan, crowds watched open-mouthed as he walked the wire for 45 minutes, making eight crossings between the towers.

As well as walking, he sat down in the middle and even lay flat on his back on the wire to chat with seagulls circling overhead.

Teamwork

The next day Petit's World Trade Center walk was front-page news all round the world. Petit was a star. The photograph opposite records the climax of a crazy adventure built on friendship, teamwork and trust.

Would You Risk It?

Could you work with dangerous animals, shin up skyscrapers or carry out daring rescue missions? Check your score on the Risk-o-meter with this easy-to-answer quiz.

1 The boat you are sailing in starts sinking. Do you:
   a Dive into the water and start swimming for shore.
   b Launch your life raft, then climb aboard.
   c Stay on board and wait to be rescued.

2 While working on a tall building you need to talk to someone at the other end of a long steel beam. Do you:
   a Jump up and down, wave your arms and shout.
   b Check your safety harness and walk slowly over to them.
   c Send them a text from your mobile phone.

3 You're a firefighter, and you see someone waving for help from the window of a burning house. Do you:
   a Immediately run into the building and up the stairs.
   b Check how bad the fire is, make a note of the address and phone for help.
   c Shout: 'Go on, jump, you'll only break a leg!'

4 You're working on a railway line in Africa when a fierce-looking lion appears. Do you:
   a Attack the lion and hope a poke in the eye will scare it off.
   b Stare hard at the lion and back away slowly. If it charges, stand your ground.
   c Run away.

5 You're working in a coal mine when suddenly the electricity shuts off, leaving you in the dark. Do you:
   a Sprint to the nearest exit.
   b Stay calm and make your way to a collection point.
   c Start screaming for help.

CHECK YOUR SCORE

Mostly a's Don't get a risky job – you'll be a danger to yourself and everyone around you!

Mostly b's You're not afraid of danger, but sensible enough to look before you leap.

Mostly c's A risky job like firefighting or being in a lifeboat crew is definitely NOT for you!

Glossary

aviation business of operating or flying planes

capsize (of boats) to overturn or sink

carbon monoxide type of poisonous gas

cave-in sudden collapse of the roof of a mine

combat readiness (of soldiers) being ready to spring into action

complicity sharing in a risky project or enterprise

daredevil person who enjoys performing dangerous stunts

distress state of a ship, plane or person in need of help

flaps parts of an aircraft wing which are lowered to help it reduce speed

girder type of steel beam used to construct buildings

illegal against the law

iron ore material used to make steel

jumbo jet large passenger aircraft

lifeboat vessel that rescues ships in trouble

logger person who fells trees

man-eater wild animal that will attack humans

migrant someone who moves from place to place

mini-sub small submarine used for undersea exploring or rescue work

Mission Control headquarters of a space mission

nuclear submarine one that carries nuclear weapons, or is nuclear-powered

photovoltaic able to convert solar radiation into electricity

propeller screw that turns to drive a sub through the water

robot machine designed to do the work of humans

rudder device used to steer a boat or ship

simulator machine for testing a plane before it flies

sound barrier speed at which sound travels

stamina strength to carry on doing something

stingray dangerous type of fish

suffocate become unable to breathe

trawler fishing boat that drags nets behind it

volatile liable to behave unpredictably

Websites

www.fireservice.co.uk/recruitment/
What it takes to become a firefighter.

www.rnli.org.uk/
Official site of the Royal National Lifeboat Institution.

www.travelmininghistory.com/index.htm
A good site about coal mining and its dangers.

science.howstuffworks.com/astronaut.htm
All about astronauts and the dangers they face.

Note to parents and teachers:

Every effort has been made by the Publishers to ensure that the websites in this book are suitable for children, that they are of the highest educational value, and that they contain no inappropriate or offensive material. However, because of the nature of the Internet, it is impossible to guarantee that the contents of these sites will not be altered. We strongly advise that Internet access is supervised by a responsible adult.

Index